P9-CRK-565

TIME SPIES

Message
in the
Mountain
A Tale of Mount Rushmore

By Candice Ransom

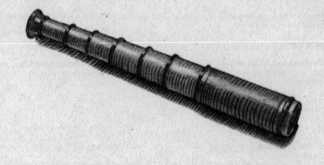

Illustrated by Greg Call

MIRRORSTONE

MESSAGE IN THE MOUNTAIN
©2008 Wizards of the Coast, Inc.

Cover and Interior art by Greg Call
First Printing: May 2008

9 8 7 6 5 4 3 2 1

ISBN: 978-0-7869-4841-3
620-21819740-001-EN

Library of Congress Cataloging-in-Publication data is on file.

U.S., CANADA,
ASIA, PACIFIC, & LATIN AMERICA
Wizards of the Coast, Inc.
P.O. Box 707
Renton, WA 98057-0707
+1-800-324-6496

EUROPEAN HEADQUARTERS
Hasbro UK Ltd
Caswell Way
Newport, Gwent NP9 0YH
GREAT BRITAIN
Please keep this address for your records

Visit our Web site at www.mirrorstonebooks.com

For Anne Bolin, my favorite innkeeper

Contents

Alex's New Brothers

Alex Chapman rolled a strip of paper into a tight scroll. With tweezers, he carefully poked it into the tube of a ballpoint pen. If this invention worked, he would have a new way to send secret messages.

"Alex, will you come to my Horsie Princess tea party?" said a voice in his ear.

Alex jumped. The tweezers clattered to the floor.

"Sophie! You made me mess up!" He

1

scowled at his sister.

"I'm sorry," said Sophie. "Can you come to my Horsie Princess tea party?"

"What's a Horsie Princess?" he asked, and then wished he hadn't. His five-year-old sister was crazy about two things. One was her stuffed elephant Ellsworth. The other was horses.

"You'll see!" She dragged Alex down the hall to her bedroom.

Arranged on the rug were Ellsworth, a toy horse, and their black and white cat, Winchester. Winchester sniffed the teacup in front of him. Everyone, including the cat, wore tiaras.

Sophie handed Alex a plastic crown. "Here. So you can be a princess too."

"Guys don't play princess." Alex glared at Winchester, who blinked sheepishly. "Some boy cat *you* are."

Sophie gave Winchester a treat. "He likes tea parties."

"He'll do anything for food." Shaking his head, Alex left.

He walked by his older sister Mattie's bedroom.

"I need to ask you something really important." Mattie held up two bead bracelets that she had made. "Which one is the prettiest? The blue one or the purple one?"

Bracelets! Horsie Princess tea parties! Alex threw his arm over his forehead and staggered backward.

"I'm outnumbered by girls! I wish I had a brother!" he said.

He thumped downstairs to the first floor. Sometimes it was hard being the only boy in the family. His father and Winchester were boys, but they didn't count. If he had a brother, they could do guy stuff.

As Alex scuffed his sneakers on the hall floor, the doorbell rang.

"Alex?" Mrs. Chapman called from the kitchen. "Will you get that? I'm up to my elbows in shortbread dough. It's probably the guests for the Jefferson Suite."

Alex bounded to the front door, his heart racing. His parents ran a bed-and-breakfast called the Gray Horse Inn. When he and Mattie and Sophie had moved to Virginia earlier that summer, they had discovered that the old house hid a secret. Hidden in the secret tower room was a magic spyglass that took them on adventures back in time! But before they went on those trips, they always met a special guest who helped send them on secret missions. This Travel Guide always stayed in the Jefferson Suite. And now the

4

new Travel Guide had arrived!

Alex jerked open the big oak door. Two women stood on the porch.

"Hello, young man," said the dark-haired woman. "I'm Shelly Layton and this is my sister Stacy."

The other woman had blond hair. "Hello!" she said. "We have reservations for the Jefferson Suite tonight."

"Are you sure?" Alex couldn't believe it. There had never been *two* Travel Guides before!

Just then someone pushed past him. It was Mattie. "Don't keep Travel Guides waiting on the porch!" she whispered. Opening the door wide, she said to the sisters, "Come in, please."

Alex scowled as Mattie swept by with the guests. Just because she was nine, a year older than he was, Mattie sometimes acted like she was queen of the world! A brother wouldn't be that bossy.

He followed the parade into the Keeping Room. His mother joined them with a tray of refreshments. Sophie bounced in with Ellsworth.

Stacy Layton strolled over to a framed picture of Thomas Jefferson that was hanging over the desk.

"That's my favorite painting of Thomas Jefferson," Mrs. Chapman said. "Since Monticello is so close, we have pictures of Jefferson all over our house."

"This is the Gilbert Stuart 'Edgehill' portrait," said Stacy. "Jefferson sat for this during his first term as president. Jefferson told Stuart he wanted to paint the hall floor of Monticello grass green. Stuart mixed up the perfect shade as a sample."

"Who'd want a green floor?" said Alex.

Shelly Layton smiled at him. "People had different tastes in Colonial days."

"Lots of our guests visit Monticello. Are you going?" Mattie asked her.

Shelly nodded. "My sister and I are art historians. Tomorrow we're giving a lecture on the artists who captured Jefferson's image in oil, marble, even crayon."

"Hey, I'll draw you a picture." Sophie fished a box of crayons and paper from under the sofa.

"I'm an artist too," said Mattie, jangling her bead bracelets. "I made these today. Which do you like best? The blue one or the purple one?"

Alex sighed. He couldn't draw a straight line and the Daniel Boone puppet he'd made in first grade looked like King Kong. He was no good at art. This mission was going to be awful. He just knew they'd be sent back in time to a boring old art museum.

"Oh, *brother*," he muttered to himself.

The next morning Alex woke up to an odd *swish*, *swish* sound. A sheet of paper was being slid beneath his door.

He jumped out of bed and opened the door. He didn't see anyone, but heard giggling around the corner. Then he picked up the paper.

It was a crayon drawing of two boys. The caption said, "Your New Brothers." Alex recognized Mattie's handwriting and Sophie's bigheaded figures.

He tossed the drawing on his desk. Mattie's idea of a joke, obviously. After pulling on jeans and a T-shirt, he went downstairs to the dining room.

When he reached the door, he stopped. Two boys sat at the table with Shelly and

Stacy Layton. No . . . the "boys" were really Mattie and Sophie! His sisters were wearing his old jeans and T-shirts. Their hair was tucked under baseball caps.

"Is the circus in town?" Alex remarked, sitting beside Sophie.

"You keep talking about wanting brothers," Mattie replied. "Now you have them."

"Ellsworth is your new brother too." Sophie showed off her stuffed elephant dressed in a little red cap.

"Very funny." Embarrassed, Alex shoveled bread pudding on his plate.

"Your sisters—I mean, *brothers*—have been telling me about your visit to Monticello earlier this summer," said Stacy Layton. "Did you notice the paintings?"

"No," Alex mumbled. He remembered the mammoth jawbone and the cannonball clock. And Jefferson's spyglass that looked just like theirs.

"Thomas Jefferson sat for many portraits," Shelly said. "But no matter how many times Jefferson was sculpted or painted, no one was able to capture his true image."

"Why didn't they get better artists?" Alex asked.

"The artists were famous," said Stacy. "The problem was that Jefferson did so many things. He was a patriot, governor, president, writer, inventor, architect—it's hard to put all of that in one painting."

Shelly spooned hash browns from the bowl. "The year before Jefferson died, a sculptor made a life mask of Jefferson's face."

"A mask?" Alex pictured Thomas Jefferson in a scary Halloween mask.

"The sculptor covered Jefferson's

face with several layers of plaster," Shelly explained. "As the plaster hardened, it began to hurt. Jefferson groaned in pain. His family was so upset, the sculptor broke the plaster off with a mallet. He put the pieces together, but Jefferson looked a little like Humpty Dumpty."

"In our lecture, we're going to discuss a sculptor who is rarely mentioned," said Stacy. "He captured Jefferson's likeness in a *really* big way—"

Alex felt a flicker of interest.

Before Stacy could finish, the kitchen door swung open and Mrs. Chapman came in with a platter of fresh sliced peaches and melon. She began to clear away the breakfast plates.

Shelly jumped up and stacked her and her sister's dishes on the tray.

"Please sit down and have more coffee,"

Mrs. Chapman told her.

"I don't mind." Shelly carried the tray into the kitchen.

"What were you starting to say," Alex asked Stacy, "about something really big?"

She checked her watch. "My sister and I need to leave. Shelly!"

A few minutes later, Shelly came out. "Is it time to go already? Bye, you *guys*."

Mattie and Sophie laughed as the Layton sisters rushed from the dining room.

"Hey!" Alex said. "They didn't write a postcard! How are we going to get our clue about where we're going?"

"It's there," said Sophie.

Alex glanced at the sideboard. Sure enough, a postcard lay in the silver tray. "How did—?"

Mattie pounced on it. "I guess Ms. Layton picked up one of our postcards," she said.

"She must have filled it out in the kitchen and put it in the tray when she came back. We just didn't notice."

Alex nodded. None of them had ever seen the Travel Guides change the photo of the Gray Horse Inn on the postcard into a new scene. But it always happened.

"What's the picture?" he asked, joining Mattie.

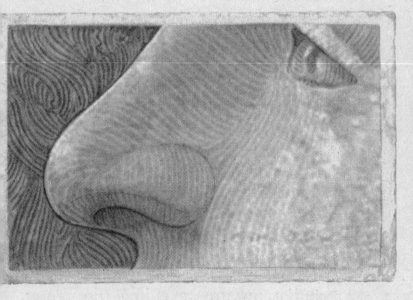

She frowned. "It looks like—a gigantic nose!"

"It *is* a nose! I bet we're going to an amusement park. No! A miniature golf course!" At least they weren't traveling to an art museum.

Mattie flipped the card over and read the message out loud.

The History of the United States by Elon Rukavina.

Alex frowned. "It sounds like a book or something."

"The postcard messages never make much sense until we're there," Mattie said. "Let's get going."

Alex led the way upstairs to the third floor. He knelt by the small bookcase and swiveled it inward, revealing the secret passage to the tower room. The others followed.

Inside, Alex removed the brass spyglass from the desk—the only piece of furniture in the room—and held it out by one end.

"Ready?" he asked.

Sophie nodded and grasped the middle. She clutched Ellsworth in her other hand.

"As many times as we've done this, I still don't like this part," Mattie said as she gripped the other end of the spyglass.

Alex closed his eyes and let the magic happen. The floor seemed to fall away from under his sneakers. Bright blue and grass green sparkles flickered behind his eyelids. As he swooped into the tunnel of colored lights, he realized something. His sisters were going back in time dressed like boys.

15

George Washington's Eyebrow

Thunk!

Alex's feet hit something hard, like a floor. But he was still *moving*. Whatever he had landed on swayed beneath him. He opened his eyes. And blinked.

He was standing on a small wooden platform with rails on three sides. The open fourth side faced rough rock. Cables attached to the rails held the platform in the air. Bright blue sky stretched high above the rock wall. Way, *way* down below tiny green trees sprouted like blades of grass. Miniature buildings were scattered near a ribbon of road. The houses and trees, Alex realized, were full size.

Mattie and Sophie stood beside him. Mattie's baseball cap was tipped forward, blocking her vision. Her hand went up to fix her cap.

Alex knew how much his sister feared heights. She would flip if she saw how high up they were. "Mattie," he said quietly. "Don't look yet."

"Why not?"

"Trust me." Alex studied the cables. Were they strong enough to hold the swinging platform and the three kids?

"Ooo!" Sophie tucked Ellsworth in her pocket and leaned over the rail. "Look at the little bitty houses down there!"

"Sophie, watch out!" Alex warned.

Mattie pushed her cap back. She gazed around with huge eyes, and then screamed. Her scream echoed for miles, startling a flock of crows.

"Quit it!" Alex said.

Mattie threw herself on the floor of the platform. "Get me out of here!"

Suddenly a voice thundered, "Hey!"

A man suspended from a cable dropped down beside them like a spider on a silk thread. He was strapped in a leather seat. A large jackhammer was clamped between his knees. The man walked his feet along the rock wall until he grazed the edge of the platform.

"What are you boys doing here?" he yelled. Before Alex could answer, the man looked up and shouted, "Winch the cage up!"

Alex looked up too and saw a small boy

18

perched on a ledge above them. The boy repeated the words, "Winch the cage up!"

With a shudder, the platform slowly crept up the mountain. Someone, somewhere, was pulling the cables that held the wooden cage. Alex and Sophie gripped the rails. Mattie flattened herself on the floor, whimpering.

The cage scraped over the top of the mountain. A man ran out of a wooden shack and tied the platform to a spike in the rock.

"You kids taking a joyride?" the man asked angrily. He shook his finger at Alex. "If the Chief finds out, you'll be fired. Lonnie's been waiting for you to relieve him." He stomped back into the shack.

Alex and Sophie stepped out of the cage. Mattie was still lying on the floor, her hands covering her eyes.

Alex gawked at the side of the mountain. Wooden stairs zigzagged up the rocky slopes. Walkways and little huts clung to the steep sides. Scaffolds strung from a network of cables were connected to other scaffolds by ladders. Men with drills dangled in leather seats, swinging out over the craggy ledges as if they were a few feet off the ground instead of hundreds. Other men scampered across the walkways and up and down the ladders.

"This is definitely not a miniature golf course," Alex said. He knew they couldn't just stand there without getting in trouble. "Get up!" he told Mattie.

She peeked between her fingers. "Give me the spyglass. I want to go home!"

"The spyglass stays in my pocket. We can't go home until we figure out our mission and do it. Get *up*. Somebody's coming!"

The boy scrabbled up the ledge on his backside, pushing with his boots. Alex noticed he wore a wide leather belt attached to a cable.

Mattie crawled off the wooden platform and struggled shakily to her feet.

When the boy was on top of the mountain, he unhooked his belt from the cable and headed toward them.

The boy was a few years older than Mattie, Alex guessed. He had thought the boy was younger because he was small and wore glasses. Rock dust powdered the boy's overalls and brown hair.

"Are you going to take root?" the boy asked Alex. "Mount Rushmore will be finished before you move."

Mount Rushmore! Alex looked at Mattie and Sophie. They were on top of the famous monument *while* it was being carved!

"All these people work here?" he asked the boy.

"Yeah. My pa is a driller. He got me a job this summer. I'm Lonnie." He stared at Alex. "You *are* the new call boy, aren't you?"

"Uh—yeah." Alex had no idea what a call boy was. "I'm Alex."

"I'm glad you're here. It's my break and the boy who usually relieves me went down the mountain sick." Lonnie stumped over the rounded crest of the mountain toward the wooden shack. "Follow me. Your brothers can wait here."

Alex and Lonnie entered through a side door into the winch house. Under the slanted ceiling, narrow windows lined the front wall. Strange machines marched in double rows along the length of the room.

Alex recognized the man who had anchored the platform earlier. He cranked a handle on one of the machines. Gears creaked and a thick cable snaked from the

machine out through a window.

"This is Charlie," Lonnie told Alex. "He's worked here in the winch house since the beginning of the project, back in twenty-seven."

Alex figured he meant 1927. He wanted to ask Lonnie what the current year was, but then Charlie yelled at them, "Where's that new call boy?"

"Right here," Lonnie said. "I wanted Alex

to see the winch house since he's new."

"Well, hurry up," Charlie grumbled.

"The winches lower and raise the drillers, the steel nippers, and the powder monkeys," Lonnie explained.

Alex had no idea what he was talking about. Steel nippers?

"But it's so noisy in the winch house that the men can't hear the workers when they ask to be pulled up or down," Lonnie continued. "Your job is to sit between the workers and the winch house and yell the orders."

They went back outside. Alex saw a big dark-haired boy sitting on the rock, his back leaning against a crate.

Lonnie saw him too and frowned. "Fred March, what are you doing here? You said you were going home sick. You don't look sick to me."

Fred took an apple from his tin lunch pail

and polished it on his sleeve. "My headache might come back."

Alex thought that Lonnie looked mad enough to spit nails. "You're supposed to relieve me when I'm on my break!"

"I need to rest." Fred bit into the apple.

"He's just plain faking!" Lonnie stalked off with Alex following behind.

They walked to the edge of the mountain, where Lonnie had left the cable. He unbuckled the wide belt he had worn and gave it to Alex. "Put this on."

Alex tried not to look down as he fastened the belt around his waist. Lonnie hooked the cable into a metal ring on the back of the belt.

"Are you sure that thing will hold?" Alex asked nervously. "It looks kind of skinny."

"The cable is steel. It won't break. Sit down and scoot down to that ledge." Lonnie pointed to a rocky seat down the mountain. "Stay there until my break is over."

"You're kidding!"

"Don't worry, it's easy." Lonnie said. "You just shout out whatever the drillers, steel nippers, or powder monkeys tell you. Remember, they're counting on you."

"But—!"

"Down you go to George Washington's eyebrow." Lonnie pushed Alex into a sitting position and nudged him over the ridge.

On his backside, Alex slid down George Washington's gigantic forehead.

Was Lonnie telling the truth? he wondered. *Would the cable really hold*?

- 3 -

Your New Brothers

The Bully

Alex braced his sneakers against the rock. He was actually sitting on the edge of George Washington's left eyebrow! The cable was taut and firmly connected to the winch behind him on the mountain.

He took a deep breath. Below him, he could see Washington's huge nose projecting from the rock wall. Four men in harness seats were working on the side of Washington's face. With their heavy jackhammers the men

27

drilled small holes in neat rows. Each man wore a number.

The driller wearing number eight on his back looked up at Alex.

"Eight up six inches!" he yelled.

Alex twisted around, cupping his hands around his mouth. "Eight up six inches!" he shouted as loud as he could.

Someone in the winch house must have heard him because Number Eight's harness began to rise. The driller called, "Whoa!"

Alex yelled, "Whoa!" and the harness stopped.

Another driller shouted, "Number Ten, need a bit!"

Alex didn't know what that meant, but he repeated the order. A man with a big leather pouch on his shoulder was lowered in a harness seat down to Number Ten. The man with a pouch took the drill bit from the driller and gave him a new one. Alex wondered if that man was the "steel nipper."

The sun beat against the mountain, bright and hot. Alex was thirsty and hungry. He wondered how long Lonnie's break lasted.

After a while the chattering drills were switched off. The four men called, "Up!" Alex relayed the command.

One by one, the drillers were raised past Alex to the top of the mountain. Moments later, another group of workers were lowered in wooden cages. They began stuffing firecrackers in the drilled holes.

When Alex saw men wiring blasting caps, he realized that the "firecrackers" were actually sticks of dynamite. Working quickly, the men packed the holes with wet sand, and then connected each hole with a series of electrical wires.

"Up!" the men chorused and Alex gave the order to the winch house.

As the workers were being raised, Alex worried about being left behind. What if they forgot about him? Suppose the dynamite went off?

But then he felt a tug on the cable hooked to his belt. The cable pulled him until he was able to stand up and walk over the ridge of George Washington's forehead.

Mattie and Sophie were waiting for him.

"I hate this mission," Mattie said, her voice quivering. "Why do we have to be up so high? What are we doing here?"

"We're on Mount Rushmore for a reason," he told her. "After we accomplish our mission—whatever it is—we can go home." He looked at her pale face and added, "I think you're being very brave."

"I don't feel brave. I feel like jelly!" She took off her cap and shook out her dark hair. "It's so *hot*."

Alex glanced beyond the winch house where the crew was sitting on crates. The workers were all either men or boys. Not a single girl.

"Matt, put your cap back on," Alex said. "And keep your hair up. You and Soph will have to pretend to be boys on this mission."

Mattie sighed, but twisted her hair up on her head and jammed her cap back on.

Lonnie came over. "You did good," he said to Alex. "I got busy in the winch house and couldn't relieve you. I haven't met your brothers."

Alex thought fast. "Uh . . . this is Matt. And this is—"

Before he could think of a boy's name for Sophie, she blurted out, "I'm Ellsworth. And this is Ellsworth the Second." She held up her stuffed elephant.

Alex shot her a look. Leave it to Sophie to make things even more confusing!

"Glad to know you," Lonnie said. "It's lunchtime. Come on."

They sat a little apart from the workers. Lonnie opened his lunch box and took out two sandwiches wrapped in newspaper.

"Pa packed too much, as usual," he said. "Will you help me eat this food?" He handed Alex one of the sandwiches.

Alex guessed that Lonnie had seen that they had nothing to eat and was being nice. "Sure. If you have enough." He divided the extra sandwich three ways.

"I haven't seen you kids before. Do you live around here?" Lonnie asked.

"Well . . ." Alex hesitated.

"I get it. You are all homeless because of hard times too."

Alex looked at Mattie. They'd heard about "hard times" before on an earlier mission. They knew that in the 1930s, during the Depression, a lot of people lost their jobs.

Alex decided to use an excuse that usually worked. "Our parents sent us to our aunt's to live. But we ran out of money. So I got a job here. When we've saved enough, we'll take a train to our aunt's."

Lonnie nodded. "Pa and I used to move around. We like living in South Dakota. He's a miner, but work got scarce at the Holy Terror Mine in Keystone."

The what mine?" asked Mattie.

"Holy Terror." Lonnie grinned. "The owner named the gold mine after his wife."

He pointed to a bearded man joking with the others. "That's my pa. His name is Theo Rukavina."

"That's an odd name," Mattie said. Alex noticed that she had pitched her voice low to sound more like a boy. "So is Lonnie."

"My real name is Elon but everybody

calls me Lonnie," he replied.

Elon! Alex thought. That was the name in the postcard message. The big nose in the picture must be George Washington's on Mount Rushmore.

"Pa and Ma came from Yugoslavia to America before I was born," Lonnie went on. "Ma died a few years ago."

"Oh, that's so sad," said Sophie. "You can hold Ellsworth the Second to make you feel better."

"That's okay. Pa and I make a good team. Pa is so proud to be a driller on the monument. To some guys, it's just money. But Pa and I feel like we're doing something real important."

Alex wished he could tell Lonnie that Mount Rushmore *was* important. It would become one of the most famous places in the United States.

"I bet you don't have a place to sleep, do you?" Lonnie asked. "Most of the workers stay in the bunkhouse down the mountain. But Pa and I rent a house in town. You're welcome to stay with us for a while."

"Thanks," Mattie said. "We'd like that."

Just then a man with a brushy mustache bustled out of the winch house. He wore a white shirt with rolled-up sleeves, a polka-dot scarf that flowed in the wind, and a cowboy hat.

"We'll set the charges later," the man told the crew. "I want the Peterson brothers, Hoot, and Palooka on Jefferson this afternoon. Fred, you're call boy."

"Who's the guy with the mustache?" Alex whispered to Lonnie.

"Mr. Gutzon Borglum," Lonnie replied. "He's the sculptor."

"What charges?" asked Mattie. "What's

he talking about?"

"The powder monkeys put dynamite in the drill holes," said Lonnie. "Everyone has to be off the mountain when they set off the charges."

"They're going to blow up the whole mountain?" Sophie's eyes were wide.

Lonnie shook his head. "The holes aren't very deep. Only one layer of rock is blasted away at a time. You heard the Chief. Let's get to work, Alex."

Alex felt a ripple of excitement. They still didn't know their mission, but he bet it had something to do with the head of Jefferson that was being carved.

As the men collected their lunch pails, someone remarked, "Game tonight. Seven o'clock."

"I'll be there!" Fred March said loudly.

"You'd better," said the man called Howdy

Peterson. "You're our best left fielder."

"What game?" Alex asked Lonnie.

"The workers have a baseball team. They're pretty good too. They play other teams around here."

"Do you play?" asked Sophie.

Fred March heard her. "Lonnie on our team? That's a good one! He throws like a girl!"

"What's wrong with the way girls throw?" said Mattie.

"Only the *men* are allowed on our team," Fred bragged. "But Lonnie can play games with you and your bear, Short Stuff." He prodded Sophie in the stomach with one finger.

Sophie's brows drew together. "Ellsworth the Second is *not* a bear! She's an elephant."

Fred sneered and snatched Ellsworth

from Sophie. He sprinted to the edge of the mountain.

"ELLLLLSWORRRRTH!" Sophie screamed.

Without thinking, Alex ran after the big boy.

"Alex!" Mattie shrieked. "Watch out!"

Fred dangled Ellsworth over the side of the mountain. "One step," he said to Alex, "and the grubby bear bites the dust."

"Give it back," Alex said firmly.

Fred pretended to drop Ellsworth. "Oopsy-daisy!"

Sophie began to cry. Alex could tell that Fred was enjoying himself. He had one chance . . . and he took it.

Kicking Fred in the shin, Alex grabbed Ellsworth just as the older boy let her go. He clutched onto the stuffed paw of the elephant and ran back to the others.

Fred hopped around, rubbing his shin. The men laughed.

"I'll get you for this," Fred told Alex through clenched teeth. "You just wait!"

- 4 -

The Contest

"Call boy!" Howdy Peterson yelled. "Get a move on!"

With a final glare at Alex, Fred limped away.

"Looks like I made an enemy," Alex said, handing Ellsworth back to Sophie.

"Fred thinks he's so great because he's on the team," Lonnie said. "Don't worry about him."

But Alex *was* worried. He wasn't afraid

of bullies—well, not *too* much—but he, Mattie, and Sophie had to find out the mission and solve it. If they had to deal with a bully, the job would be even harder.

"Do you and Alex have to go back to work?" Mattie asked Lonnie.

"Another call boy is taking this shift. Would you like to see the place?"

"Yeah!" said Alex.

Lonnie led them past the winch house over the crest of Jefferson's egg-shaped head. Mattie walked slowly, never lifting her eyes from the granite surface.

"Matt, are you afraid of heights?" Lonnie asked.

She nodded, hanging on to her cap in the strong, gusty wind.

"It's nothing to be ashamed of," said Lonnie. "Lots of workers quit after their first day, or even their first trip up here. We're five hundred feet from the ground."

Mattie looked like she was going to faint, so Alex said quickly, "When will Jefferson be finished?"

"Hard to say. We lost eighteen months on the old Jefferson head."

"How many heads does Jefferson have?" Mattie asked.

"Mr. Borglum wanted to put Jefferson on the left side of George Washington." Lonnie waved his arm toward the far end of the mountain. "The men began drilling, but the rock was too crumbly. So Mr. Borglum had the old Jefferson face blasted off. They started the new one here, on the right side of Washington."

Alex rubbed the toe of his shoe on the rock. It was as smooth as a sidewalk. "How long have they been carving Mount Rushmore?"

"Seven years. Pa started last summer. This is my first summer."

Alex remembered that Lonnie had said that work began in 1927. That meant it was now 1934.

"How come everybody isn't working on Jefferson?" Sophie wanted to know.

"Mr. Borglum decides what we work on every day," Lonnie replied. "A few men are still finishing Washington's collar, shoulder, and arm."

"Jefferson is the most important," said Alex. Then he added, "I mean, besides Lincoln and Roosevelt. And Washington." He didn't want Lonnie to think they had special connections to Thomas Jefferson.

"Jefferson *is* important," Lonnie said. "Pa and the other drillers blasted sixty feet of surface rock on the new Jefferson head just to find rock they could carve. He told me they could run into problems at any time. And if they do, well, they might call off the whole project. We could all lose our jobs."

"What are those things?" Sophie was staring at a round metal plate on top of Jefferson's head, not far from where they were standing.

A tall pole rose from the plate and was supported by cables. A horizontal steel beam was fastened to the plate and wires hung off the end of the beam. An identical device was mounted on Washington's head.

"That's Mr. Borglum's pointing machine," Lonnie replied. "It helps the workers make measurements. Mr. Borglum has a model of the presidents in his studio. An inch on the model equals a foot on the mountain."

Alex nodded. "I saw a miniature house once. It was made to scale. One inch was the same as one foot, so it looked exactly the same, only smaller. You can build anything that way."

"That metal plate turns, so the beam can swing around," Lonnie explained. "There are metal weights on the end of the wires that are pulled up and down. The men take measurements from them."

"I'm hot," said Mattie. "We must be closer to the sun or something."

"We'll go to the bottom now." Lonnie led the way across the top of Jefferson's head to a ladder and began climbing down.

Mattie threw Alex a scared glance. Alex knew going down is worse than going up when you are afraid of heights.

"Matt, you go after Lonnie," he said. "So—uh, *Ellsworth*, you're next. Give me Ellsworth the Second so you can use both hands."

Carefully, they climbed down the ladder

to a short ramp. At the end of the platform more steps clung to the mountain. They climbed and climbed. On one of the ramps, they stopped to catch their breath.

"I've never seen so many stairs in my life!" Alex panted.

"Over seven hundred," Lonnie said. "Plus forty-five ramps. I know, because I climb them every morning. It takes thirty minutes to get to the top of the mountain."

Mattie pointed to a wooden car gliding along a cable up the side of the mountain. "How come we can't ride in that?"

"The tram is mostly used to haul tools," Lonnie told them. "Some of the workers ride in it. Call boys walk."

They continued down until they stood on solid ground again. Alex felt relieved.

Several outbuildings were clustered at the bottom of Mount Rushmore. Lonnie showed them the bunkhouse, where most of the workers stayed. The rest lived in Keystone, the nearby town.

Next they visited the blacksmith's shop. The brawny blacksmith explained that all the drill bits had to be sharpened every day.

"The mountain chews up the bits," the blacksmith told them. "It's made of hard, tough granite. The drill bits have to be replaced after they are used to drill about three feet."

Lonnie took them to the building where the air compressors that ran the jackhammers were stored and the hoist shack that housed the machine that operated the tram.

Lonnie put his finger to his lips as they approached the last building, a log cabin. "If you're quiet, he won't yell at us."

"Who won't yell at us?" Alex said, but

Lonnie had already pushed open a large door.

The building was filled with light from large windows. Tools hung from nails and large plaster masks were propped along the rough walls. In the middle of the floor rose a large statue of four men.

Alex recognized the faces of George Washington, Thomas Jefferson, and Abraham Lincoln. The fourth figure wore glasses and

a mustache. Alex figured that was Theodore Roosevelt.

The figures were carved to the waist. Alex could see the buttons on George Washington's coat and the wrinkles in his sleeve where his arm was bent.

Gutzon Borglum stood on a ladder leaning against Lincoln's shoulder. He scribbled in a notebook and muttered to himself.

Then Sophie sneezed from the dust. The sculptor glanced down and frowned at them.

"I don't recall inviting visitors," he said.

"Sorry." Lonnie hurried them out. "He's in a good mood today. He didn't get real mad."

"What was that statue?" Mattie asked.

"That's Mr. Borglum's model. He checks measurements with it all the time."

"The statue showed the presidents' clothes and arms and stuff," said Alex.

"Yeah," said Lonnie. "They dedicated George Washington's head a few years ago, but he's still not finished."

"But—" Alex stopped himself. He knew that only the heads of Mount Rushmore were ever carved into the mountain. For some reason, the sculpture had never been finished. But Lonnie wasn't supposed to know that.

Lonnie waved at a bare section of the mountain. "You see that smooth part over there? Mr. Borglum was going to carve a tablet in the shape of the Louisiana Purchase.

He had the year seventeen seventy-six carved on it, the year of the Declaration of Independence. You could see the numbers from three miles away."

"What happened?" asked Mattie. "It's gone."

"They blasted it off," Lonnie said, "because they had to move Jefferson's head.

Now Lincoln has to go in that spot."

Alex was watching the men scurry down the ladders, catwalks, and steps. "What's going on?"

"Work is over for today," Lonnie said.

One of the men carried a fuse box and unrolled wire from a big spool. "All clear?" the man yelled.

A young man in a blue shirt checked a list on a clipboard. He nodded. "All off the mountain."

The man with the fuse box pushed the plunger. With an ear-splitting *bang*, a giant cloud of dust, rocks, and boulders slid down the side of the mountain.

"Wow!" Alex said. "That was better than the Fourth of July! How come the whole mountain didn't fall down?"

"Only the rock we want to come off is blasted away," said a new voice. A tall man with brown eyes like Lonnie's loped over. "Ready to go home, Lonnie?"

"Yes, Pa. This is Alex, Matt, and Ellsworth Chapman. They need a place to stay for a few days. I said they could bunk with us."

"Stay as long as you need to," said Mr. Rukavina. He walked over to an old-fashioned car and turned the handle on the back. Instead of revealing a trunk, he pulled up a seat! "You kids hop in the rumble seat," he said.

Alex, Mattie, and Sophie scrambled into the open backseat. Alex looked over at the mountain. A small figure scrambled up the rock pile at the bottom. It looked like Fred March, but Alex couldn't be sure.

Lonnie climbed in the passenger seat beside his father and they took off, chugging down the bumpy road. They drove a short distance to a small town.

Parking the car next to an unpainted house, Mr. Rukavina led everyone inside.

He fixed a simple supper of beans, bologna, and bread. The kids washed the dishes.

"Time for the game," Lonnie's father said. "Let's go watch."

They walked over to a baseball field where some of the workers were pitching and catching balls. Fred March wore a shirt with "Rushmore Memorials" on the front and the number nine on the back.

"He's not supposed to wear the uniform to a practice game," Lonnie said. "He's just showing off."

Just then Mr. Borglum strode into the center of the field.

"I have an announcement!" he said. Everyone fell silent. "I'm going to move the entablature to the back of the monument.

It will be across from the Hall of Records, a cave I'm designing."

"What's an entabla-whatever?" Alex whispered to Lonnie.

"The stone tablet I was telling you about," Lonnie whispered back.

Mr. Borglum went on. "The Hall of Records and the entablature will cover the history of the United States. That will be the message of this mountain! The famous newspaper publisher, William Randolph Hearst, is sponsoring a contest to write the history of the United States in five hundred words."

Alex thought that was a pretty dull. Even guessing the number of jelly beans in a jar was more thrilling. But Lonnie's face shone with excitement.

"Among the judges are President Franklin Roosevelt and First Lady Eleanor Roosevelt!" said Mr. Borglum. "Anyone can enter! There will be prizes—cash and a college scholarship."

"I wish I could go to college," Lonnie said. "Nobody in my family ever has."

Alex looked at him. Maybe their mission was to help Lonnie.

"Why don't you enter the contest?" he said.

"I don't know about history!" Lonnie said. "I haven't had much schooling because Pa and I move around a lot."

Fred March overheard them as he headed for the outfield. "That's right. Lonnie's too dumb to enter that contest. Dumb and weak. He throws like a girl."

Lonnie turned on his heel and walked away.

"I think I know what our mission is," Mattie said to Alex and Sophie. "We need to get Lonnie to enter that contest. He needs our help to get a college scholarship."

Alex glared at Fred March in the outfield. "I think we're supposed to put that bully Fred March in his place."

Sophie shook her head. "No. Our mission is Jefferson."

"What about Jefferson?" Alex asked her.

But Sophie wouldn't say any more.

- 5 -

History Helpers

Lonnie ran up to the Chapmans. "How about a soda pop? My dad said we could go into town."

"Yeah!" said Alex.

Alex, Mattie, Sophie, and Lonnie left the baseball field and walked into Keystone. First Street was lined with small businesses and a lot of black cars like Mr. Rukavina's.

"Tourists," Lonnie said. "They come here to watch the workers on Mount Rushmore."

58

He led them into a grocery store.

Alex had never seen a store like this. Shelves were piled with everything from rubber boots to frying pans.

Lonnie fished around in a metal cooler filled with cold water. "Do you like Strawberry Nehi?" He pulled out a small dripping bottle and handed it to Alex.

Alex pried off the cap with the opener and drank. "Boy, that's really fizzy!" *Sodas taste better back in the old days*, he thought. The cars were *definitely* better. He kind of liked 1934.

They went back outside and sat in rocking chairs on the store's front porch.

"Over there is the entrance to the Holy Terror Mine." Lonnie waved his bottle toward a large wooden building. "Where Pa used to work."

"I'd rather work in a gold mine than on

top of Mount Rushmore," Mattie said.

"No way!" Alex rocked back and forth in his chair. He remembered their mission to the Yukon, where they tried to help Mike Harding pan for gold in a riverbed. "Finding gold is hard!"

Lonnie nodded. "And Mount Rushmore pays better. I make twenty-five cents a day as a call boy. Besides that mine has ghosts!"

"Ghosts?" Alex stopped rocking.

"Sometimes men get killed in cave-ins. People say their ghosts drift through town after dark."

Alex shivered and not just because the night air was chilly. He didn't like the sound of ghost miners running around.

"But isn't it just as dangerous to work on Mount Rushmore?" Mattie asked.

"There hasn't been a single accident," said Lonnie. "Though on Pa's first day, he thought he was a goner. He was being low-ered in the harness chair for the very first time. All of a sudden he dropped like the cable had broken! Then he stopped. The men up top were laughing. They play that joke on all the new workers."

"What's so funny about that?" said Mattie.

Alex gazed up at Mount Rushmore. From this distance, he could see the maze of scaffolds, ramps, stairs, catwalks, sheds, and cables. George Washington's deep-set eyes were shadowed, but he still appeared noble.

"I don't understand how the mountain is being carved," he said. "Some guys drill holes and then the rock is blown off. But how did George Washington *get* there?"

"Pa explained it to me," Lonnie said. "The rock is blasted off a layer at a time until you can see the shape of the head. Next, the drillers carve the big features like the eyes, ears, and nose."

"They carve it with jackhammers and dynamite?" Alex asked.

"Yeah, but the holes they drill are close together, so not much rock is blasted away. After the main features have been carved out, then the bumpers get to work. They're the guys who actually use a hammer and chisel to 'bump' off the last chunks. They make the carving look smooth and lifelike."

"How come Mr. Borglum picked these presidents?" Sophie asked.

"Well," Lonnie said. "George Washington is the father of our country. Thomas Jefferson wrote the Declaration of Independence. Abraham Lincoln saved the country during the Civil War."

"What about Theodore Roosevelt?" asked Alex. "What's so special about him?"

"Some people don't think Roosevelt is that important, but Mr. Borglum wouldn't give in," Lonnie replied. "He says Roosevelt belongs on the monument because he helped get the Panama Canal finished."

"That doesn't seem so important," said Mattie.

"The Panama Canal connects the Atlantic and Pacific oceans, so people don't have to sail all the way around South America any more."

"Wow, I didn't know all that." Alex said. "Hey, you know a lot about history."

Mattie nodded. "You really should enter that contest. I bet you could win."

Lonnie shrugged and placed his empty soda bottle in the crate by the store's front door. "Better head home."

In the house, Lonnie and the kids put the

dishes away while Lonnie's father read a newspaper in the next room.

"Guess we might as well go to bed," Lonnie said.

"What about your essay?" Mattie asked. Alex knew what she was thinking. They needed to get started on their mission. But was the essay their mission? He still wasn't sure.

Mattie grabbed a tablet and pencil from the kitchen counter and sat next to Lonnie. "You just need to write down all that stuff you told us about the presidents and the Panama Canal."

Lonnie sighed. "I know stuff about the monument, but I don't know everything that happened in history."

"We'll help you," Mattie said. "All you have to do is write five hundred words. You can't put everything in history in it. Only the really important things."

"Yeah," Alex said. "Like televi—" Mattie jabbed him with her elbow. He had almost said *television*, which probably wasn't even invented yet.

"Start with the pilgrims," Mattie suggested. "How they came over on the *Mayflower* and stepped on Plymouth Rock."

Lonnie scribbled for a while. Then Mattie and Alex read over what he had written.

"Not bad," said Alex.

"It's a good start," Mattie added.

Mr. Rukavina stuck his head in the doorway. "It's late. We have to get up early for work tomorrow."

Lonnie showed the kids the room they would share. It had two beds and a mattress on the floor for Sophie.

Sophie curled up on the mattress and fell asleep right away, but Alex and Mattie talked a while.

"I can't climb that horrible mountain again," Mattie whispered. "Do you think we could go home soon?"

"I wish we could, Matt," Alex said. "But we're still not positive about our mission."

"I'm sure we're supposed to help Lonnie win the contest." She yawned. "All he has to do is finish his essay tomorrow and then we can use the spyglass and get back home."

"I guess." Alex punched his pillow. He was glad to help Lonnie with his essay. But was that really their mission? Something didn't feel right.

Just as Alex was dropping off to sleep, he heard Sophie mumble something as she turned over. It sounded like "Jefferson's nose."

6

A Secret Is Revealed

Someone was shaking his shoulder. Alex rolled away.

"Get up, sleepyhead," said Lonnie. "We have to be on the mountain by seven. Pa fixed toast."

Minutes later, Alex, Mattie, and Sophie were dressed and eating slices of jelly toast. When they heard the car engine sputter to life, they hurried out the door behind Lonnie. The Chapmans piled in the rumble seat and they all rattled up the road to Mount Rushmore.

At the bottom of the monument, a line of men filed up the stairs. The tram, filled with equipment, was being hoisted up the side of the mountain.

"Seven hundred steps," Mattie said grimly.

It took much longer to climb up Mount Rushmore than it did to walk down. At the top, a young man wearing a crisp green shirt met them. Alex remembered the man who had checked off names on a clipboard at the end of the workday.

"Hello," the man said to Alex. "I don't know you."

Alex swallowed. "I'm Alex Chapman. The new call boy?"

"I don't remember hiring a new call boy, but I suppose my father did. I can use you," the young man said. "I'm Lincoln Borglum. You and Lonnie will go with the Jefferson crew this morning."

Fred March pushed through the line. "I'm on Jefferson, Mr. Borglum. I'm always call boy on Jefferson."

Lincoln Borglum glared at him. "Do you run this project?"

"No, sir." Fred seemed to shrink.

"I want you on Washington today," Lincoln Borglum told Fred. "Now."

"What about *those* other kids?" Fred jerked his thumb at Mattie and Sophie.

"I'll handle the employees around here." After Fred stomped off, Lincoln Borglum asked Mattie, "Who are you?"

"I'm—Matt Chapman, Alex's brother," she replied. "And this is Ellsworth, our little brother."

Lincoln Borglum frowned. "Why are you

two on this mountain?"

"I'm a—a substitute call boy," Mattie said. "You can use me in case somebody faints or something."

"And Ellsworth? Is he here in case the substitute call boy faints?"

Alex put his hand on Sophie's shoulder. "Ellsworth is too young to be left at home. And we don't have any parents." That was partly true. They had left their parents back at the Gray Horse Inn, in the future.

Lincoln Borglum sighed. "All right. Matt and Ellsworth, stay out of the way. Lonnie and Alex, get to work."

Alex followed Lonnie to the winch house. Ahead of them, Fred practically closed the door in Lonnie's face.

What is he so mad about? Alex wondered.

As they picked up their safety belts,

Lonnie asked Alex, "Will you help me with my essay again tonight?"

"Sure." Alex noticed Fred taking more time than necessary to pick up his belt. He was sure the older boy was listening to them.

The drillers were busy climbing into harnesses. Gripping their jackhammers, they walked backward over the side of Jefferson's head. Alex was ordered to sit just above Jefferson's unfinished nose, while Lonnie was assigned to an area just above Jefferson's right cheek. Before Alex could strap on his belt, a voice boomed out.

"Hold it!"

Gutzon Borglum, polka-dot scarf flapping, strode over to a leather harness. A winch man carefully lowered the sculptor over Jefferson's face. Dipping a brush into a small can of red paint, he made marks on

Jefferson's left eyebrow.

"Bump it down another two inches," he said to some men on top.

Lonnie explained to Alex, "Mr. Borglum wants the carvers to take more rock off the eyebrow. He makes changes all the time. He looks at the mountain in the morning and afternoon. He even looks at it through binoculars from Iron Mountain, four miles away."

"Why does he do that?" Alex asked.

"To see how the sunlight and shadows fall on the carvings," Lonnie replied. "The Chief wants the heads to be real art."

"How come you call him the Chief?" Alex asked.

"Because he's the boss. But we don't say that name so he can hear it."

As Alex and Lonnie buckled their belts, Mattie and Sophie walked toward them.

Alex felt a prickle of annoyance. *What are*

they doing here? Didn't Lincoln Borglum tell them to stay out of the way?

Suddenly a puff of wind blustered across the mountain. The wind yanked Mattie and Sophie's hats off. Their hair tumbled loose.

Lonnie gaped at them.

Alex's heart dropped like a driller in a harness chair. The secret was out.

7

Sounds in the Night

"You're—you're *girls*!" Lonnie exclaimed. "Who are you?"

"These are my sisters, Mattie and Sophie," Alex said.

Lonnie whirled on Alex. "How come they're going around as *boys*?"

Mattie stuffed her hair back under her cap. "We didn't see any women working on Mount Rushmore. So Sophie and I pretended to be boys."

74

"We're on an important mission." Alex admitted to Lonnie.

Lonnie's eyes grew round. "What kind of a mission?"

"We can't tell you," Alex said.

"Please don't give us away." Mattie put Sophie's cap on her head and tucked her little sister's hair beneath it.

"I won't." Then Lonnie said, "I hope you'll tell me what's going on when you can."

"Why did you come over here?" Alex asked Mattie. "Mr. Borglum told you and Sophie to stay out of the way."

"We heard Fred March say he was going to get you," Mattie said. "He's telling everyone that you took his job on the Jefferson crew. That guy's got it in for you and Lonnie. You'd better watch out."

"He's not nice. He tried to throw Ellsworth

off the mountain!" Sophie sounded indignant.

"You can't get any lower than that." Alex chuckled. He wasn't afraid of bullies like Fred—well, not *too* much.

Once Alex began working, he forgot about the older boy. Jackhammers echoed like a hundred woodpeckers. Drillers shouted to be lifted or lowered or to have fresh bits delivered. A great monument was being created and Alex was part of it!

At the end of their four-hour shift, Lonnie and Alex switched places with two other call boys. Alex shook hands with the boys he hadn't met. They seemed okay. Only Fred March was a bad egg.

Lincoln Borglum came over with his clipboard. "Lonnie, you're on the morning shift tomorrow. And Alex, you'll take the afternoon."

Since Lonnie's father was working a double shift that day, the kids stayed on the mountain until four o'clock.

The more sure-footed men "billy-goated" down the mountain, sometimes skipping a dozen steps, as they rushed to the bottom. Alex and the others walked down carefully.

Back at the Rukavinas' house, the kids helped Lonnie finish his contest essay.

Mattie read it over one last time. "It's perfect!" she said. "Now, all you have to do is turn it in tomorrow and we're done."

"Done with what?" Lonnie asked.

But Alex knew what she meant. Once Lonnie turned in his essay, their mission would be complete.

Luckily Mattie didn't have to explain because Mr. Rukavina came in and told them all to go to bed.

Alex was so tired that he fell asleep right

away. It seemed to be only minutes later when he opened one eye.

Screek. *Scrape*.

Alex sat up in bed. *What was that*? It sounded like an object being dragged along the floor. *Could it be a rat*? he wondered. Maybe he should go check.

Then Alex remembered the ghosts from the Holy Terror Mine. What if a *ghost* were in the house? He decided to stay in bed and pulled the sheet over his head. The noises soon stopped and he went to sleep again.

- 8 -

Tracking a Rat

Lonnie burst into the Chapmans' room. "It's gone!"

"What's gone?" Alex asked.

They were dressed. Mattie was tucking Sophie's hair under her cap.

"My contest entry!" Lonnie cried. "I left it on the table. It's not there now."

"Are you sure?" Mattie said. "Maybe your father moved it."

Lonnie shook his head. "I asked him. He

said he never saw it."

"Let's look around," said Alex.

They checked the windows, which were closed to keep out the chilly night air. The windows were locked, except for a small window in an empty back room.

"That one's stuck, nobody can get it open," Lonnie said.

"At least we know the wind didn't blow the papers away," Alex said.

When the others left to eat breakfast, Alex checked the stuck window. He couldn't budge it. Then he examined the window frame. In a few places, the wood was dented. The marks looked bright, as if a sharp tool had scratched them into the wood.

"Alex!" Sophie called from the kitchen. "Mattie says your oatmeal is getting cold."

Mattie was pacing around the table. "What are we going to do?"

Lonnie sat at the table with his head in his hands. "I only made one copy. I'll never be able to write it over. I can't remember it."

Mr. Rukavina came in and picked up his lunch box. "Don't fret about it now, son. I'll help you tonight. But now we have to report to work."

"You might as well stay here," Lonnie said to Alex. "You're not on till after lunch." He left with his father, his shoulders sagging.

When the car had chugged away, Mattie turned to Alex. "We have to find that essay or our mission will be ruined. What if we can't get back home?"

Alex sighed. "I feel terrible. I heard noises last night, but I didn't get up to see what they were. I thought it was a rat."

"It *was* a rat," said Sophie. "A big one."

Alex nodded, catching on. "You mean a great big rat named Fred March? Do you

81

think he sneaked in here and stole Lonnie's essay?"

Sophie nodded.

"I think Soph might be right," Mattie said. "But how did he get in? The windows and doors were locked."

"Let's walk over to the bunkhouse and look for clues. It's not that far," said Alex.

"Good idea," Mattie said. "Everybody will be at work."

The kids walked along the road toward Mount Rushmore. Several cars passed them. Some were parked by a sign that read, "A View of the Monument, Information, and Souvenirs." People sat on the hoods of their cars, peering at the mountain through binoculars.

"This place is already a tourist stop," Mattie remarked. "And it's not even half finished."

"It *is* an awesome sight," Alex said. He gazed up at Jefferson's profile. Something tugged at him from the corner of his mind, but he couldn't remember what.

The bunkhouse was empty. Rows of wooden bunks lined both walls. At the end of each bed stood a footlocker.

"How will we know which bunk is Fred's?" Mattie asked.

"Look for something of his," said Alex. Then he spied the shirt draped over the bedpost of an unmade bunk. It said, "Rushmore Memorials" on the front. The number nine was written on the back.

"That's Fred's," said Sophie.

"This must be his bed," Mattie said. "Check the foot locker."

Alex figured the trunk would be locked, but the lid lifted easily. Inside were clothes, shoes, and an extra blanket, but no essay.

"Nothing here," he said.

Mattie was on her knees, poking under the bed. "I found something." She hauled out a wooden box filled with chunks of light gray granite. "Why would Fred keep a box of rocks under his bed? He's not the type to collect rocks."

Alex picked up a piece of cardboard that had fallen out of the box. He read the card and frowned. "No, but he's the type to collect *money*."

He held out the card, which read, "Rare Rocks, Two Dollars." After rooting through the rocks Alex pulled out a leather pouch. Undoing the drawstring, he poured dollar bills and coins on the floor.

Mattie whistled. "That's a lot of money! I didn't think call boys made that much."

"They don't." Alex looked inside the pouch and saw a note curled up at the bottom. He pulled it out and read it aloud. " 'Ma, I'll send more when I can.' "

Alex scooped the cash back inside the pouch. "Fred is up to something. Maybe he's selling rocks from the Holy Terror Mine, telling people these rocks are gold."

Sophie poked one of the small rocks. "They don't sparkle like gold."

"I'll take one as a sample." Alex slipped the small rock in his pocket. "Maybe we'll find more like it."

Mattie shoved the box back under the bed. "Lonnie's essay isn't here. We'd better go before somebody comes in."

Outside, they wandered around the sheds and buildings. Then it was time for Alex to leave for his shift.

"Jefferson's nose," Sophie said sadly.

Alex turned to her. That's what he was trying to remember. She had spoken those words in her sleep. "What about Jefferson's nose?" he asked Sophie.

"It's going to fall off."

9

Sophie to the Rescue

"What do you mean?" Alex said. "His nose is part of the mountain. It can't fall off!"

"Yes, it can." Sophie insisted.

Alex remembered the postcard the Travel Guides had left them. "Mattie! What if the nose in the postcard picture is *Jefferson's*? Suppose there *is* something wrong with the Jefferson carving, and that's our real mission?"

"What are you talking about?" Mattie said. "Our mission is the essay."

"Yeah, but remember what Lonnie said? The rock where Jefferson's head was supposed to go was too crumbly. The same thing could happen to this head too." Alex fingered the rock in his pocket. "I have a feeling Fred is mixed up in this somehow. We need to find out the truth."

"How are we going to do that?" Mattie asked.

He pointed to the top of the mountain. "There's only one way."

Alex peered around the corner of Gutzon Borglum's studio. It was after four o'clock. He, Mattie, and Sophie had walked down the mountain after Alex's shift as fast as they had dared.

Now they hid behind the log cabin, waiting for the powder monkeys to set off the dynamite charges. Alex watched some men unload crowbars, jackhammers, and other tools from the tramcar.

Kabloom! B*oom*!

Rocks and rubble flowed down the mountain, kicking up a huge dust cloud. When the dust settled, Alex motioned for Mattie and Sophie to follow him.

"Where do you think *you're* going?" said a familiar voice.

Alex spun around. "Lonnie! We thought that you'd gone home with your father."

"He's playing cards in the bunkhouse with some friends." Lonnie looked at them suspiciously. "How come you're sneaking around Mr. Borglum's studio?"

Alex glanced at Mattie. She nodded. They could trust Lonnie.

"Remember when I said we were on a mission?" Alex told Lonnie. "It has to do with the Jefferson head. We think there's something wrong with it."

"Like what?" Lonnie looked confused.

Sophie spoke up. "His nose is going to fall off."

"Pa has drilled on the new Jefferson head from the beginning," said Lonnie. "He'd know if anything were wrong."

"Has he worked on Jefferson's nose?" Alex asked.

"No." Lonnie shook his head. "He can't stand Fred and Fred's usually the call boy on Jeffer—" He broke off. "Fred's in on this, isn't he?"

"Maybe." Alex showed Lonnie the rock sample. "Is this rock from the mountain?"

"Yeah. It's granite."

"Fred is selling these rocks," Mattie said. "We think he knows something we don't."

"We need to check Jefferson," Alex said.

Lonnie shook his head. "Not by yourself.

You don't know how to run the equipment. I can help."

"Okay," Alex said. Lonnie was right—none of them knew how to operate the winches.

"Let's hurry," said Mattie. "It gets dark fast once the sun sets. I don't want to come down that mountain in the dark."

Alex eyed the tram. "We'd go up a lot faster if we could use that."

"Somebody would see us," Lonnie pointed out. "We'll have to walk up. Keep low and we won't be spotted."

They crept up the stairs. By the time they reached the top, Alex's knees hurt from walking crouched over.

"You lower me in the harness," Lonnie said.

Alex shook his head. "I have to do it. It's the way the missions work."

"Then Mattie and I will lower you. Sophie,

can you be the call boy? Can you yell good and loud?"

She nodded.

Lonnie went into the winch house and returned with a harness, and a call boy's belt. He pulled two cables behind him that were reeling through the windows. Mattie and Lonnie helped Alex into the leather harness. Lonnie fastened the straps.

"Mr. Borglum designed this contraption himself," Lonnie said. "You can't fall out, even if you get conked on the head."

"I hope that doesn't happen." Alex checked the steel cable, just in case.

Next Lonnie buckled the belt around Sophie. He clipped the second cable to the ring on the back of the belt.

"Okay," he said. "Mattie, you'll control the cable that holds Sophie. I'll take care of Alex."

"You mean, I have to operate that winch thing by myself?" Mattie asked.

"You can do it," Alex told her. "Look how brave you have been, climbing the mountain and walking around up here."

Next Mattie and Lonnie guided Sophie to the edge of Jefferson's forehead. Sophie sat down, her short legs over the side. Alex was amazed that his little sister wasn't the least bit afraid.

He grasped the arm straps and stood on the ledge over Jefferson's nose, facing backward. "I'm ready," he said, even though he really wasn't.

Mattie and Lonnie ran over the crest of Jefferson's head and disappeared into the winch house. After a few minutes, the cable on Sophie's belt tightened. Alex knew Mattie had control of the winch supporting Sophie.

"Lonnie says to walk back!" Sophie called.

Alex took a hesitant step backward. Then two more steps. One more . . . and then he felt the world drop beneath him. This wasn't like the feeling he experienced when the spyglass sent them back in time. This was scary! But the cable held and he was secure in the harness, though he kept swinging away from the mountain.

"Use your feet!" Sophie ordered.

Alex knew Lonnie was relaying directions to Sophie from the winch house, but it still felt weird having his five-year-old sister telling him what to do. He grabbed the rough rock with his shoes, pulling himself closer to the wall.

The cable began to move. Alex let himself be lowered, sometimes falling jerkily, sometimes walking down the wall. Finally he hung below Jefferson's nose. Alex pictured the stone Thomas Jefferson blowing his nose on a handkerchief the size of a football field.

Pay attention, he said to himself. But what was he looking *for*? The rock appeared to be just . . . rock. Maybe he needed to check someplace else.

"Sophie!" he yelled. "Tell Lonnie to raise me about two feet!"

Sophie repeated the order.

Alex gripped the arm straps, preparing to be lifted. The cable shifted, but instead of being raised, Alex was dragged sideways. The cable snagged on the tip of Jefferson's nose!

"Sophie!" he shouted. "I'm caught!"

Seconds later, Sophie reported, "Lonnie says the winch is stuck!"

Stuck! Panic rose in Alex's throat. What if Lonnie couldn't free the cable? Would he have to hang there until work began the next morning?

Then he noticed something. The evening shadows stretched over Jefferson's nose, highlighting the rock on the right side. A dark line ran through the end of Jefferson's nose.

A crack!

Suddenly, all the clues fell into place. The rocks, Jefferson's nose, everything. He had to tell someone. Fast.

"Sophie!" he cried. "Pull me up!"

Sophie relayed his message and the cable slowly raised him upward. Alex clambered up the side of the mountain. He passed Sophie who still sat on the edge of Jefferson's forehead.

Near the top, he stubbed his toe and lost his balance. He swung out wildly on the cable.

"Help!"

Sophie scooted along the ledge until she could grab one of Alex's harness straps. She hung on to him so he would stop moving.

Then he heard footsteps on the rock above. A rope with a loop at the end was flung over the edge. Alex clutched the rope with both hands. The harness began to rise again. Soon he was able to scramble over the side.

"Are you okay?" Mattie bent over him.

"Yeah," he said. "Sophie saved me."

"So did Mattie. She's got quite a throwing arm," Lonnie said as he hauled Sophie to the top of the mountain. "She could be on the Rushmore Memorials team."

"What did you find?" Mattie asked him.

"A crack." Alex shrugged out of the harness. "It's underneath. I don't think you can see it in the daylight."

"We'll tell Pa and he'll tell Mr. Borglum," Lonnie said.

"No, you won't," a voice said.

The three kids turned and saw Fred March coming toward them. His fingers clenched a rock, ready to throw it at Alex.

10

Jefferson's Nose

"I wouldn't do that if I were you," Alex warned. "I know what you did."

Fred's mouth twisted into a sneer. "You're bluffing. You don't know anything."

Alex pulled the small rock from the bunkhouse out of his pocket. "You've been on the mountain in the evenings collecting these plain old rocks to sell to tourists."

"So what if people want to buy rocks from Mount Rushmore?" Fred said. "It's no crime."

"No, but it shows how desperate you are for money." Alex said.

A dark red flush crept up Fred's neck. "Keep your nose out of my business!"

"Jefferson's nose is our business," said Alex. "When you were collecting rocks up here in the evenings to sell, you saw the crack in Jefferson's nose. But you didn't say anything."

"It's not my fault." Fred kicked the rubble at his feet. "Mr. Borglum has a terrible temper. He fires people over the least little thing. If I told him about the crack, he'd be so angry that he would fire me. Or he might have to shut down the whole project! And my ma really needs the money."

"Is that why you didn't want anyone else working on Jefferson?" Lonnie asked. "You were afraid another call boy might see the crack and the work would shut down?"

"Yeah, maybe."

"But there's more, isn't there?" Alex didn't take his eyes off Fred. "You broke into Lonnie's house and took his contest essay, didn't you? You opened the back window with a crowbar. The marks are still bright where you scratched the wood."

"You and dumb, weak Lonnie needed to learn a lesson. You took my place on Jefferson, so I took your paper." Fred dug a much-folded piece of paper from a side pocket of his overalls.

"My essay!" Lonnie exclaimed.

Fred jerked the paper back. "I'll let you have it on one condition—you keep quiet about all of this."

"Listen, Fred," Alex said. "We have to tell someone about the crack in Jefferson's nose."

"Or the nose will fall off!" Sophie piped in.

Alex nodded. "But if you give Lonnie his paper, we won't tell Mr. Borglum that you

101

knew about it and kept it a secret."

Fred glowered at Lonnie.

"Now," Alex said.

Reluctantly, Fred handed Lonnie the essay.

As they hurried toward the bunkhouse, Mattie said to Alex, "Nice going! You got the paper without promising to keep quiet."

"He won't get away with it," Alex said. "I'll fix him somehow."

With Lonnie in the lead, they burst into the bunkhouse. Lonnie's father and several men were playing cards around a table.

"Lonnie," Mr. Rukavina said, getting to his feet. "What is it?"

"We have to talk to you, Pa. Outside."

Puzzled, Lonnie's father followed the kids out behind the bunkhouse.

"There's a crack in Jefferson's nose," Alex began. "Maybe a blast did it or something."

"What?" The big man stared at him. "How do you know this? Have you kids been up on the mountain?"

"I can't explain, but I wouldn't bother you if I wasn't sure," Alex answered.

Mr. Rukavina glanced up. "A crack would fill with ice in the winter, and then thaw in the spring. Over time, the crack would get bigger and eventually it would damage Jefferson's head. We must tell Mr. Borglum right away. You kids stay here."

Alex and the others waited while Lonnie's father knocked on the door of Mr. Borglum's office. Moments later, the sculptor burst out, along with Lincoln Borglum and Mr. Rukavina.

"Get the crew out here!" Mr. Borglum ordered. "Prepare the tram and stand by. I'll need two men to operate winches on top. Move!"

Mr. Rukavina and Lonnie scurried to the bunkhouse. Soon men were running around everywhere. Two men started the engine in the hoist house. Mr. Borglum, Lincoln, Jesse Tucker, and Lonnie's father boarded the tramcar.

Alex, Mattie, Sophie, and Lonnie watched the tram glide up the cable to the top of the mountain. Mr. Rukavina and the other worker rushed into the winch house. Soon Mr. Borglum and Lincoln were lowered in harness chairs over Jefferson's head.

People from Keystone and tourists gathered at the base of the mountain. They pointed at the men in the harness chairs swinging from the giant nose.

"Word gets around fast here," Alex said to Lonnie.

"It's a small place," Lonnie said. "Mount Rushmore is the biggest thing for miles around. I think it's the real reason people come to South Dakota."

Fred March brought his crate of rocks from the bunkhouse and set up the sign.

"Can I find some rocks too?" Sophie asked.

"Okay, but don't wander off too far," Alex told her.

They were all quiet as they watched Mr. Borglum and Lincoln walk up and down the stone nose, and then signal to be raised again. When the tram touched down, everyone dashed over. Mr. Borglum climbed out first.

"It has come to my attention," he said in his booming voice, "that there is a fissure along Jefferson's nose. I have no intention of leaving a head on this mountain that, in the course of five hundred or five thousand years, will be without a nose."

The crowd murmured as the sculptor stalked over to his studio and went inside, slamming the door.

"What's he going to do?" Alex asked.

"Figure out how to fix it," Lonnie said.

The tourists and townspeople milled around the job site. Fred March tried to snare their attention.

"Mount Rushmore rocks from the damaged Jefferson head!" he cried. "Only two dollars for a rare rock!"

Mattie started laughing. "Look at Sophie!"

Sophie stood behind an upturned wooden box. The top of the box was covered with pebbles. A piece of cardboard proclaimed, "Rox Free."

People clustered around Sophie's souvenir stand. No one browsed Fred March's rock collection. Alex imagined that he could almost see the steam pouring out of Fred's ears.

Alex grinned at his little sister. "Way to go, Soph."

At last the office door banged open and the sculptor came outside.

"I have the solution," he said. "I will shift the measuring device back four feet and tilt the head eighteen inches. The facial features will be rotated five degrees north."

"How can he move the head?" Mattie asked. "It's part of the mountain!"

"He hasn't carved the features yet," said Lonnie. "Only the beginning of the nose."

Mr. Borglum was still talking. "The crack will now run through Jefferson's right eye, past his nose and upper lip and through his chin. The mass of the mountain will support the carving. We'll fill the crack with a mixture of granite dust, white lead, and linseed oil to keep water out."

The workers tossed their caps in the air and cheered. Mr. Rukavina clapped his hand on Lonnie's shoulder.

"The work will go on," he said, smiling. "This monument will be finished."

At his words, Alex realized that they had completed their mission.

"That's it," he whispered to Mattie. "We helped Lonnie write his contest essay. And we helped get Jefferson's nose fixed so it won't fall off."

"And Sophie put Fred March in his place!" Mattie ran over to Sophie and brought her back. "We're ready to go home."

Alex pulled the spyglass from his pocket. He held the spyglass by one end. Sophie clasped the middle and Mattie clung gratefully to the other end.

Alex felt the ground give way beneath his feet. Flecks of green and blue swirled behind his eyelids. Then—

Whoomp!

His sneakers hit the solid floor of the tower room. Mattie and Sophie appeared beside him.

"You're both covered with granite dust!" he said.

"So are you," Mattie told him. "We'd better clean up before we go downstairs."

They took turns brushing off one another's clothes.

"You and Soph were pretty good actors," Alex said. "Everybody thought you were really my brothers. But I like you better as my sisters."

"Really?" said Sophie.

"Yeah, you're both awesome," Alex admitted. "Mattie, you showed me that there

109

is nothing wrong with the way girls throw. And Sophie, you saved Jefferson's nose—and me!"

"And she got back at Fred March!" Mattie said. "Sophie was the star of this mission!"

Walking over to the desk, Mattie took the envelope from the drawer, and then headed for the bookcase-panel.

Alex stowed the spyglass in its box. "Do you think we have a book about Mount Rushmore downstairs? I wonder if Lonnie's essay won the contest."

"Maybe we'll learn more in the Travel Guides' letter." Mattie disappeared through the bookcase-panel.

Alex started to follow her when he noticed Sophie lingering by the desk. She cradled Ellsworth in the crook of one arm and studied something that she held between her thumb and index finger.

"Soph?" he asked. "What are you doing?"

"Nothing. I'm coming."

Plunk.

She dropped a pebble into an open drawer.

Alex blinked. The pebble was light gray, the same color as the granite on Thomas Jefferson's nose.

Or was it?

Dear Mattie, Alex, and Sophie:

Or should we say, "Dear Matt, Alex, and Ellsworth?" You all handled the challenges of time travel well this time.

The sculptor you met, Gutzon Borglum, was born in Idaho in 1867. His large-scale statues include Seated Lincoln and Wars of America. He began carving Southern generals of the Civil War on Stone Mountain in Georgia. He didn't get along with the committee who hired him and was later fired.

Then Borglum was asked to create a monument on another mountain. At 5,725 feet, Mount Rushmore is one of the tallest mountains in the Black Hills region of South Dakota. Instead of portraying Western heroes, such as Lewis and Clark and Buffalo Bill, Borglum chose to honor presidents. "America will march along that skyline," Borglum said. He briefly considered Susan B. Anthony, a leader for women's rights, but stuck with Washington, Lincoln, Jefferson, and Theodore Roosevelt.

Work began in October 1927. Over the years, nearly four hundred workers drilled, blasted, hammered, chipped, and chiseled the granite mountain. The workers blasted a half million tons of rock. Several times the project stopped because there wasn't enough money to pay the workers and buy supplies. Work also halted during the long bitter winters.

Over a period of twenty years, workers scrambled up and down ladders to heights that equaled a forty-story building. They swung from harness seats and set off dynamite charges. Yet there were no deaths and only minor injuries.

Originally Gutzon Borglum wanted to carve the full figures of the presidents. When he died in March 1941, his son Lincoln took over. The project ended in October 1941 with only the heads completed. Congress refused to give anymore funds to the Mount Rushmore monument. America was about to enter World War II.

The Hall of Records, the cave on the back of the mountain, was never finished either. Gutzon Borglum had planned the cave to have rooms lined with busts of other notable Americans, such as Benjamin Franklin and the Wright brothers. Records of America's history would be sealed in watertight capsules.

One hundred thousand entries were submitted to the essay contest advertised in Hearst's newspapers. I'm sorry to say your friend Lonnie's did not win. A young man named William Burkett won the college-age category. In 1975, Burkett's winning essay was inscribed on a bronze tablet and placed at the site of Borglum's studio.

Of all the heads, Jefferson's proved to be the most difficult to carve. In 1939 workers had to repair a six-inch chunk of loose granite on Jefferson's upper lip. That was the only patch on the entire monument—quite a feat considering the heads are sixty feet high, the same height as a six-story building! The monument is four hundred feet high and five hundred feet across. The president's noses are about twenty feet long and their mouths are eighteen feet wide.

The Native Americans who once owned the Black Hills are also getting recognition. In 1948, sculptor Korczak Ziolkowski began a memorial seventeen miles from Mount Rushmore. His enormous statue honors Lakota Chief Crazy Horse. Ziolkowski died in 1982, but today his wife and some of his children and grandchildren continue the work.

On your next trip, you will help save another presidential image!

Yours in Time,
Ms. Layton and Ms. Layton